W9-CAD-782

The Essential Guide

Written by
Glenn Dakin

HAPPY FEET™

The Essential Guide

Contents

Introduction 8
Emperor Nation 10
Baby Mumble 12
Mumble 14
Gloria 16
Memphis and Norma Jean 18
Noah and the Elders 20
The Great Guin 22
Singing School 24
Graduation Day 26
Adelie Land 28
The Unknown 30
Adventure 32
Ramon 36
The Adelies 38
Lovelace 40
Alien Invaders 42
Antarctic Life 44
The Zoo 46
The Finale 48
Acknowledgments 50

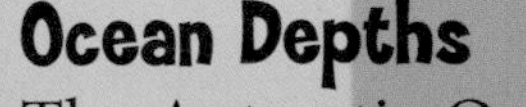

Ocean Depths

The Antarctic Ocean is typically 2½ miles (4.5 km) deep. Its lowest point is 4½ miles (7.2 km) at the South Sandwich Trench. That's one deep sandwich! The ocean ranges in temperature from 28 to 50°F (–2 to 10°C).

How low can you go?

- Orcas can dive 100 ft (30 m) in search of prey, such as fish, seals, penguins, and other whales.

- Adelie penguins aren't deep divers, but they can swim to a depth of 600 ft (175 m) when seeking food for their young.

- Emperor penguins dive down over 800 ft (250 m) when hunting for food.

- Flat icebergs, the kind that break away from ice shelves, often sink to more than 1,000 ft (300 m) deep.

- More unstable icebergs, which have splintered away from glaciers, can reach a depth of 1,600 ft (500 m).

Introduction

Get ready to huddle—you're about to enter Antarctica, the coldest place on Earth! On the southernmost point of our world is a land of extremes—none of them nice. Bitter cold, cruel winds, and four months of darkness a year sound harsh enough for you? On a barren ice shelf in this frozen land live a colony of Emperor penguins. Every year, a new generation is born into this deep-freeze, with plenty of reasons to feel grouchy at the cold welcome waiting for them. And yet, this year, one penguin called Mumble is so happy to be alive, he just can't keep still...

Emperor Nation

The unique birds that live in the Antarctic near the South Pole might look cute and quirky—but they have made a life for themselves in the harshest climate there is. In fact, you're looking at the toughest bunch of little birds on Earth! However, hard times can create hard attitudes, and the colony can be a pretty chilly place for outsiders.

"Who's the guy with the wacky feet?"

Same old, same cold

The Emperor penguins can only survive the long cruel winter if all the penguins think and act the same. For example, the Great Huddle just wouldn't work if selfish guys stayed in the middle all the time, where it's toastiest! These penguins are used to things being done a certain way, and this is why they give misfits like Mumble a hard time for being different.

As they grow older, chicks hang out together in large "creches"

The future

Memphis and Norma Jean are two of Emperor Nation's inhabitants. Each penguin in Emperor Nation has its own unique Heartsong. When two penguins' songs merge together, they fall in love. Memphis and Norma Jean's song became love and their love became a baby penguin called Mumble.

Colonies can contain 20,000 penguin pairs

Meet the Emperor

Emperors are the largest breed of penguin. They grow up to 3½ ft (1.1 m) tall and weigh up to 65 lb (30 kg). They eat mainly krill, fish, and squid and can live for up to 40 years.

THE GREAT HUDDLE
Penguins crowd together to survive temperatures of -76°F (-60°C), in winds of 125 miles (200 km) per hour. They take turns shuffling from the coldest spaces on the outside of the huddle into the middle, where they can save body heat.

Because the males don't leave the huddle to feed, they lose about half their body weight during the winter months.

"When I'm dancing, I have

Baby Mumble

This sweet ball of fluff is Mumble, Memphis and Norma Jean's baby. He may be cute, but he has one big problem—he can't sing a note to save his life! Songs are vital to penguin life, because without a Heartsong they can't find a soul mate. Luckily, Mumble has a special talent that makes up for his weak warble.

Cute face markings remind grown-up penguins to treat chicks as infants, not rival adults

Penguin chicks are covered in soft, downy feathers

Egg Scramble

Trust Mumble to be different and to try to come out of the egg feetfirst! He was named Mumble because of the muffled squawking he made while running around with a big shell on his head.

happy feet!"

Pa pressure

Mumble sure is delighted to see his dad—and his feet are happy too, so happy they can't stop hippity-hopping! Disapproving Dad tells Mumble to forget the fancy footwork and behave like a regular penguin.

Webbed feet provide perfect balance for tap-dancing

Out of tune

Somebody has to be at the bottom of the class when it comes to singing, but no penguin has ever sunk as low as Mumble. What future can such a catastrophic crooner have?

Mumble's favourite meal

Mom's fish supper

Here's how it's made:

1 First, Mom goes fishing for about nine weeks

2 Next, Mom must pre-eat the supper!

3 Then, she has to bring it back across miles of ice

4 Now at home, she throws it back up as a nice sloppy mush, which is called "regurgitating"

5 it's ready to serve! Best served chilled—say, at minus 58°F (50°C)—on an icy ridge

Can they really dance?

Penguins don't really boogie like Mumble, but they do perform a mating dance when the season arrives. This performance involves a long stare, some bowing, groovy neck swaying, and plenty of canoodling, beak to beak!

"It's like singing with

Mumble

As Mumble grows up, he longs to fit in, but the world appears to have no place for him. He is unpopular at school, where the in-crowd labels him a "weirdo." But life is going to take him on a journey that will transform him into a real hero.

As penguins grow they develop "torpedo" shaped bodies—ideal for speedy swimming

Growing pains

He always did stand out in a crowd, but Mumble is easier to spot than ever when he keeps his baby fluff and cute cheek markings after all his classmates have grown into a cool new look. Deep down though, he's every bit as grown-up as they are.

Mumble

Breed: Emperor penguin

Best Friends: Gloria and the Adelie amigos

Likes: Hearing Gloria sing

Dislikes: Hearing himself sing!

Motto: Don't ask me to change...'cuz i can't

Quote: "I'm being spontan-uous."

your feet!"

Growing up

Penguins aren't really grown-up and ready to be independent until they grow their sleek, shiny adult feathers. Unlike the soft, warm baby-down they're born with, these new feathers are waterproof. From six months to a year, penguins gradually become equipped to take to the sea and hunt fish.

Big noise

Under the glow of the Southern Lights, Gloria, the singing star, steals the show at the end-of-school concert. Then one unique voice hits the air and astounds everyone... by ruining the whole thing! Mumble does have a special gift, but it certainly isn't his voice.

Poles apart

Feeling rejected, a lonely Mumble wanders away from the penguin party. Will he ever get a chance to show everyone what he can do? Can one little bird hope to find happiness in a cold world?

"As if you're not totally

Gloria

Baby Gloria will lose her gray face feathers as she grows up

This singing sensation of the South Pole wows the wildlife with her stunning voice. Admired by all the boys on the block, she could have her pick of the penguins, but would rather hang out with her pal Mumble. Her special talent will always turn a frozen wasteland into a Boogie Wonderland!

Cute chick

Even as a fluffy toddler, Gloria was a bright spark, naming Mumble when he was still stuck inside his egg. At Penguin Elementary School, she was one of the first to discover her beautiful Heartsong.

Gloria's Guide To Guys

A real man will:

Fetch you a fish

There's nothing more romantic than the boy of your dreams bringing you a nice slimy cod in his beak.

Make romantic gestures

A really cool guy can do a fancy dive and leave a trail of bubbles in the shape of a heart.

Follow his heart

A real man will follow his own dreams, even when everyone else seems to be against him. It takes bravery, a strong heart, and the love of a beautiful woman!

There from the start

Gloria knew Mumble before he was born—it was her playful curiosity that first stirred him into life, when she tapped on his egg with her beak and he tapped back with his happy feet. She's had a special place in his life ever since.

thrilled tha

Penguin tongues are covered with tiny spikes to help them catch fish

Short, strong wings enable penguins to dive to nearly 1,000 ft (300 m)

Teen G

As Mis
the cu
she w
Glor
ser
du

Who is Gloria's Favorite Guy?

Seymour?

Charming, confident, cool—Seymour thinks he's all of these! Better at rapping than he is at sweet talk.

Lovelace?

How many guys make you pay hard pebbles to talk to them? A great date if you're prepared to queue to meet him!

Ramon?

Would be a great lover if he could get over his love affair with himself!

Mumble?

Gloria's only got one thing to say about this hippity hoppity hunk—and that's back off, ladies! His dance card is already filled.

“I love you

Memphis and Norma Jean

This passionate penguin pair brings hot love into an icy world, and Mumble is the result of their duetting. But even these proud parents are going to have their flippers full with their boogie-mad baby.

Dedicated dad

While the mothers head off to catch fish, it’s the fathers that do “egg time.” Memphis has always had a velvety voice and a sway in his hips, but an egg time accident shakes his confidence.

Memphis keeps their egg warm between his legs until it hatches

Heartbreak hotel

In the middle of egg time, Memphis has a sudden urge to boogie. In one reckless rockin’ moment, he breaks the strict penguin rule: “Never ever, no matter what, drop thy egg!”

more and more!"

It just ain't penguin!

Memphis wants his son to be "normal" and tells him to stop dancing. He is convinced that Mumble's "happy feet" are his fault for dropping Mumble when he was an egg.

Cool mama

She's got a wiggle in her walk and a giggle in her talk and Memphis is crazy about her! Mumble also adores his mama, especially the way she throws up his favorite fish dinner for him.

Memphis

Breed: Emperor penguin

Favorite Pastime: Being a rock 'n roll role model to Mumble

Pet Peeve: Dropping eggs!

Motto: The word "triumph" starts with "try" and ends with a great big "UMPH!"

Quote: "He's not different!"

Norma Jean

Breed: Emperor penguin

Favorite Pastime: Holding flippers with Memphis

Pet Peeve: Being away on long fishing trips

Motto: Make every moment count

Quote: "So what if he's a little different. I always kind of liked different."

Waterproof feathers keep skin dry

"Heed the wisdom,"

Noah and the Elders

In lean and uncertain times, the Emperor penguins in Mumble's colony turn to their Elders for the wisdom that will bring survival. Now, with fish in short supply, the "Scarcity" threatens them all. Will the old ways save the tribe, or is it time to try out some brand-new ideas?

Rulers and regulations

The penguin Elders are proud of their colony's traditions. They learn the old chants, practice trying to look wise, and try not to have an original thought or new idea.

Archaic Noah

Noah is the oldest of the Emperors and a strong leader. He is troubled by the "Scarcity" and is convinced that Mumble's "happy feet" are to blame. Noah believes in the Great Guin and refuses to accept the existence of "Aliens"—intelligent creatures from the outside world who interfere with penguin life.

Noah

Breed: Emperor penguin

Best Friend: Eggbert

Likes: Being a waddling windbag

Dislikes: Unholy displays of backsliding (otherwise known as penguins enjoying themselves!)

Motto: Stay true to our old ways

Quote: "Only the Great Guin has the power to give and take away!"

brothers!”

The cold shoulder

The Elders exile Mumble from their land becaus he won't stop dancing. But the positive penguin isn't downhearted. He sees leaving his home as a chance to go out into the world and find a way t save the very penguins who are driving him awa

Did you know that the oldest penguin on record was 27 years old? (That's 108 in penguin years!)

Penguin LAW

ou think you could handle life a penguin? It's a pretty chilly gime under the old, cold laws f Noah and the Elders—take a ook at these rules for hanging out in the winter huddle.

1

Make a huddle, and warm thy egg.

2

Share the cold!

3

Each must take his turn against the icy blast if we are to survive the endless night!

4

Give praise to the great Guin, who puts songs in our hearts and fish in our bellies.

5

No dancing—under any circumstances!

6

Never, ever, no matter what, drop thy egg!

The Great Guin

Emperor penguins in Mumble's colony believe that the Great Guin has watched over them for countless generations. This ancient spirit has put food in their bellies and songs in their hearts. But now, fish have become scarce and the Elders are frightened. Have the penguins angered the Great Guin? What must they do to satisfy their god?

An angry god?

Mumble is considered a "bad egg" because of his dancing and lack of a Heartsong. On top of that, he hangs out with party-loving penguins from other colonies! The Elders proclaim that Mumble has offended the Great Guin, who has withheld his bounty of fish. They banish Mumble to please their god and bring prosperity back to the Emperor Nation.

The huddle is always on the move. Birds take turns occupying the coldest spaces on the outside.

Mumble's colony believes that the Great Guin is their traditional protective spirit.

The penguins in the outside row of the huddle turn their backs to the cold wind.

Singing School

"Just

The most important lesson at Penguin Elementary School is How To Find Your Heartsong. But the teacher, Miss Viola, can't do it for you—you have to find it all by yourself. Listen carefully, and a voice deep inside will reveal the song that tells you who you truly are! Unless, of course, you're a certain penguin named Mumble....

Spreading your flippers expands your chest and makes for a stronger voice

Heartsong heartbreak

Mumble's lesson gets off to a bad start when he tells the teacher that the most important thing for a penguin to learn is "don't eat yellow snow." When Miss Viola invites him to sing his Heartsong, the class receives an unpleasant surprise. Mumble's off-tune bellowing may be good for dislodging icicles, but it sure doesn't sound like singing!

Vocal Miss Viola

Miss Viola usually loves the special moment when her pupils first share their unique songs with the world. Of course, there are bound to be some rotten first attempts, but Mumble's is the worst ever! A penguin without a Heartsong, she points out, is hardly a penguin at all!

be spontaneous!"

Penguin calls can be heard half a mile (1 km) away. Mrs. Astrakhan's voice can be heard slightly farther!

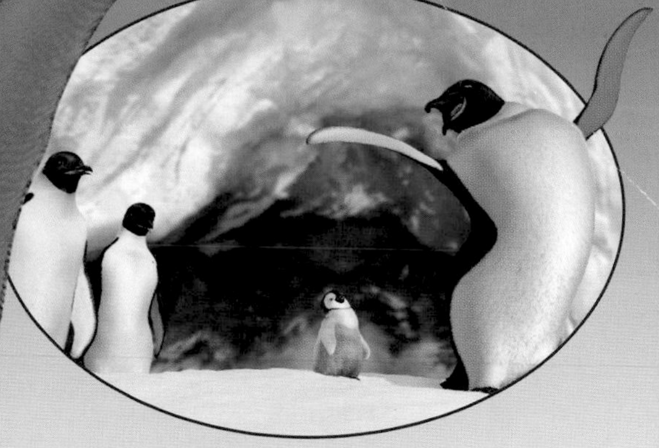

Emergency measures
Without a Heartsong, Mumble's whole life could be ruined. It's only through singing that penguins find that special someone to have an egg with! Mumble's disastrous droning forces his anxious parents to seek out the expert advice of Russian voice coach supreme Mrs. Astrakhan.

"Can't seenk? Nonsense, darlink!"
Mrs. Astrakhan helps Mumble to reach deep inside and unleash the most enormous feeling. But, unfortunately, it comes out through his feet instead of his beak! It's simply a "CATASTROFF, darlink."

Mrs. Astrakhan

Breed: Emperor penguin

Favorite Pastime: Unlocking penguin potential

Best Friend: Miss Viola

Pet Peeve: Pupils who "jiggy-jog" instead of "sink!"

Motto: If anyone can, Mrs. Astrakhan can

Quote: "Every little penguin has a sonk!"

Feet must be still during singing lessons

Graduation Day

This ceremony celebrates the moment when young penguins become adults. It can be a tough time for some—and nothing could be tougher than listening to Noah's boring speech. Still, the Elders have a point. It is kind of cool that, a thousand generations ago, the penguin forefathers exchanged their wings for flippers, and the sea became their playground!

Mumble's own ceremony

Because he hasn't found his Heartsong, Mumble isn't allowed to graduate with his classmates. Norma Jean suggests that they throw their own private ceremony for Mumble and encourages him to join his classmates as they venture out to sea.

Mumble's tail helps him steer when he's swimming

Dive right in!

That first dive from the ice cliffs into the sea is a great moment in any young penguin's life. Even the usual show-offs like Seymour are a teeny bit nervous before taking the plunge. The surprise of the day is that Mumble leads the way!

Once Mumble has taken the first dive, the graduates soon follow

The awesome Antarctic

"It's fantastic! Whatcha waiting for?" shouts Mumble, when he gets his first swim in the sea. But his father, Memphis, worries about the perils of hungry Leopard seals and Killer whales on the prowl. He warns Mumble that strangers equal danger!

Sitting target

Life seems pretty lonely for Mumble, waking up the morning after the graduation party, stranded on a piece of ice. A visit from a hungry Leopard seal doesn't exactly cheer him up—but it does lead to him making some cool new friends!

Adelie Land

Mumble enters a whole new world when a team of tiny, all-day party penguins leads him into Adelie Land. Here, the fun-loving flipper birds actually approve of dancing, and Mumble's happy feet make him a cool character. Led by a groovy guru called Lovelace, and not by a frosty fossil like Noah, the Adelies make Mumble feel like he fits in somewhere at last.

Adelie facts

- Adelies grow to 27½ in (70 cm) high and have jet-black heads with white rings around their eyes.
- They make nests of pebbles and often steal stones from each other to build them.
- Both males and females share the duty of incubating their eggs and caring for their chicks.
- Adelies mostly eat krill and their main predators are Skua birds and Leopard seals.

At nesting time Adelies march inland to their traditional rookery sites

Mumble on the case

What do you do when you discover a weird Alien machine in an ice cavern beneath your home? Forget about it as soon as possible, according to the Adelies! But Mumble insists that this mystery must be solved, so there is only one place to go—to Lovelace, the all-knowing Rockhopper penguin, on his tower of power!

Mambo, Mambo!"

Tougher Adelies fight for nest space in the middle of the colony, where they are safer from Skua birds.

Each nest contains two eggs

Guru guide
Lovelace leads Mumble and his amigos to the Forbidden Shore, where he says that his Sacred Talisman was "bestowed" on him.

The Unknown

The truth is out there. The disappearing fish, the strange Alien artifacts, the giant Annihilator machines—Mumble is sure that they're all tied together in some way. Against unknown danger, one brave bird is finally ready to demand some answers.

To boldly waddle

Beyond the Land of the Elephant Seals and out to the Forbidden Shore, this group of fearless penguins (some more fearless than others) must venture where no sensible bird would ever dare to waddle.

reception

ome to the Blizzard Country, ost unfriendly environment rth—aside from standing d an Elephant seal when een eating kelp. With icy and snowballs blowing e tumbleweeds it's no ise that the Adelies are ng to get cold feet about whole adventure!

"Let me tell something

Ramon

Ramon can be identified by his crest of light feathers

He's the smartest, coolest, best-looking Adelie in Adelie Land—well that's what he thinks anyway. Ramon is the wise-cracking leader of the Adelies, a group of penguin pals that would be real losers if they didn't have each other!

Short beak, partly covered with feathers to keep out the cold

Big ideas

Ramon thinks his impressive size can be daunting—but the only big thing about this reduced-sized Romeo is his ego! No wonder his amigos joke that his big penguin head is blocking the sun!

Ramon

Breed: Adelie penguin

Favorite Pastime: Hangin' with his amigos

Best Friends: Lombardo, Nester, Rinaldo, Raul, and Mumble

Motto: Leave 'em wanting more

Quote: "We got personality! With a capital 'Y'! Why? Because we're hot!"

to you."

Meeting Mumble

Soft-hearted Ramon spots that Mumble is all alone, so he invites him to join the gang. Mumble's bigger size and soft feathers mean that he is quickly nicknamed Tall Boy, Stretch, and Fluffy. Ramon uses the dance moves he learns from Mumble to try and lure the chicas!

Accidentally cool!

Ramon and his gang love Mumble, especially the fact that he is so "accidentally cool." Mumble leads the Adelies on the best toboggan ride ever when his tap-dancing causes the icy mountain top to crack beneath him, sending him sliding down the icy slope with his amigos close behind him.

Ramon's chick chat

1

Don't be so snooty, booty!

2

Just a moment, I hear people wanting something... ME!

Hey, I like big tails!

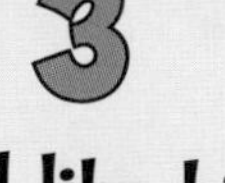

Hey baby, girly girl!

I know size can be daunting, but don't be afraid! I LOVE YOU!

The Adelies

Viva la party! Their food chain may have gone loco, but even in the bad times this gang of Latino Adelie penguins still knows how to party! Collectively, these amigos have a short attention span, but they are fiercely loyal to Mumble and join him on his wild adventures.

Lombardo

Lombardo is impressed with Mumble's dancing and thinks that his moves must have the penguin ladies drooling at his feet.

Nestor

Gifted with a beautiful voice, Nestor could bring tears to anyone's eyes as he sings of Mumble's sad exile from his homeland. Well, anyone except grouchy old Noah.

Rinaldo

Rinaldo is a crazy thrill-seeker and the first to body surf after Mumble down the steep mountainside. He will follow his pals through any danger but even he gets cold feet at the thought of visiting the Forbidden Shore.

Join the gang!

The Adelies invite Mumble to be an amigo because he's an outsider just like they are. They love the way his feet go "clickety-clickety," and make him feel accepted for who he truly is!

Raul

Raul is the rap star of the gang, breaking into his hip-hop rhymes to get the welcome attention of the chicas. However, he's a little less welcoming of an unexpected hug from Ramon!

A narrow white ring circles the eye and gives them that wide-awake look

Adelies have the best example of classic "tuxedo" style plumage

Lovelace

“Okay

Guru and self-proclaimed love-god, Lovelace uses his charisma and direct link to the Mystic Beings to become rich and adored. But when Lovelace chokes on his Sacred Talisman, Mumble discovers his secret – he never met the Aliens! Lovelace is a fraud!

Lovelace's "powers" come from this Sacred Talisman

You gotta problem? Go and ask Lovelace. There is nothing that the Guru doesn't know the answer to after he consults with the Mystic Beings. But, please, one at a time.

Lovelace

Breed: Rockhopper

Favorite Pastime: Being adored

Best Friends: His female entourage and Mumble, of course!

Pet Peeve: A dinner date with an orca

Motto: Separate the truth from the jive!

ladies, w

Long crests of feathers look like wild eyebrows

Everything about Lovelace is larger than life, including his stomach!

The Great Gu
This righteous
with his words
when Mumble
take him straig

Ice-cool love nes
The penguin with
has his pick of the
a ready-made l

Lovelace's Wise Words

1
Ladies please avert your eyes, 'cause I've been known to hypnotize.

2
Why don't we all go forth and multiply?

3
Don't touch the talisman, baby!

4
There's not enough love in the world!

5
Turn to the penguin next to you. Put your flippers up–fluff him up a little bit–and give him a great big hug.

6
I'm gonna be telling your story Happy Feet, long after you dead and gone.

Alien Invaders

Some call the Aliens the Annihilators because it is believed that they take penguins and turn them into mush, then they stomp on the mush and suck it up through a straw! Others refuse to believe that they exist at all. Mumble is about to find out the terrifying truth...

Is anybody there?

After all the myths and rumors, Mumble finally proves that the Aliens exist, when he leads Lovelace and the Adelies to the Forbidden Shore.

Brave Mumble walks ahead to investigate the Alien's building

The whaling station

Hooks, chains, and blubber slicers may be Alien technology to penguins, but they sure get the general idea. As Ramon points out, it's definitely not a come-right-on-in kind of place!

Enormous hull full of fish

The whaling ship

Rising a hundred feet out of the sea and churning the pack-ice before it, the great black ship fills the hearts of the heroic penguins with dread.

Loco-maniac!

When they witness the awesome metal monster that is taking their fish, the Adelies and Lovelace naturally think they've reached the end of the line. But Mumble is determined to see his quest through to the end, so he dives off a towering iceberg in pursuit.

In deep water

The plucky penguin gambles everything on trying to contact the Aliens inside the ships to ask them why the fish are disappearing. But he fails and is left to drift at the mercy of the tides. After swimming until he is exhausted, Mumble passes out and is washed up on a distant beach.

When he dives off the iceberg, Mumble loses his fluffy feathers. By the time he hits the ocean, he's wearing sleek swimming feathers

Mumble swims after the ship for as long as he can, but loses it in the vast ocean

Antarctic Life

Mumble shares his icy backyard with some pretty cool creatures, but, like all penguins, he has to be careful because not all the neighbors are friendly. Basically, if you're not planning to eat them, they're planning to eat you!

Skewered by Skuas

The food chain is very simple to the sneaky Skuas. Flipper birds eat fish, and flying birds eat flipper birds and the fish! Lately there haven't been a lot of fish. That's unlucky for the flipper birds.

Leopard seals have long, sharp teeth for cutting and tearing prey apart

Come here, supper!

Mumble loses a tail feather or two to the snapping jaws of the Leopard seal, but wows the admiring Adelies with his speedy escape.

Elephant
can weigh
to 4 tons!

An Orca's
curve inw
and backw
keep a tigh
on prey

Other Penguins

Who's had all the krill? Emperor penguins are not short of colorful competitors when it comes to searching the seas for a good meal.

Krill—these tiny shrimp are eaten by many Antarctic animals.

MACARONI PENGUIN
Easily recognized by their bright yellow-and-orange crests, these grow to 30 in (70 cm) high.

CHINSTRAP PENGUIN
These feisty birds are named after the black bands of feathers that run under their bills.

KING PENGUIN
The second largest penguin, and a close relative of the Emperor penguin, can be recognized by their bright orange ear patches.

GENTOO PENGUIN
This tough bird can swim faster than any other penguin, up to 22 miles (36 km) per hour.

The Zoo

After Mumble is rescued from the beach, he discovers that there really are Aliens that look like big ugly penguins with flabby faces and frontways eyes. They have put Mumble in a zoo with other penguins, but a zoo is no place for a talented tap-dancing flipper bird!

Awestruck audience: The sea-life center observation gallery is full of humans transfixed by Mumble's dancing

Alien language?

Mumble can see the Aliens, but they can't understand a word he's saying. That's weird, because he's speaking plain penguin. He just wants to know why they're taking all the fish!

Mumble is front-page news—luckily, penguins look good in black and white!

First contact

Mumble loses all hope, until a little girl taps on his window. The beat reawakens something special in Mumble's heart—and his happy feet start hippety-hopping again.

The dancing penguin

Suddenly Mumble's feet are doing the talking, and at last the human world is paying attention. Scientists want to find out more about this toe-tapping wonder, so they send Mumble home hooked up to a tracking device.

BOOGIE BIRD BAFFLES BRAINS

One little penguin is making a big splash and sending ripples through the scientific world. When visitors to this sea-life center tap on the glass, this sensational seabird taps back—with his feet! The big question everyone is asking here is: Where did this astonishing creature come from? It is vital that steps be taken to protect the lives of all

Wash a
up on
arctic if
beach a
and resc
penguin
with a
also o
in a
Ha

The Finale

Mumble's return plunges Emperor Land into crisis. Is he a traitor as Noah says? Or is he a hero who can save them all? It's time for the penguins to choose their next steps wisely.

Mumble's message

The waddling wanderer has a message for his people. Yes, the Aliens are taking our fish, but they have the power to make things right again. Mumble explains that the only way to communicate with them is by dancing!

Flippers help Emperors keep their balance while boogieing down

dance now!"

Alien landing

The old order is overthrown when a noisy helicopter lands in the middle of Emperor Nation. Noah is forced to admit that he is wrong and that Aliens really do exist.

Show me whatcha got!

What's gotten into the penguins—is it some kind of disease? No, it's a tap-dancing penguin extravaganza! The humans don't understand the sudden change in penguin behavior, but they sure don't want it to stop. As governments lay down plans to limit fishing to protect this amazing species, our hero Mumble has solved the mystery behind the missing fish and helped the penguins dance their way to a brighter tomorrow.

Mumble's sleek tuxedo look is perfect for an evening of ice-dancing with Gloria

LONDON, NEW YORK, MUNICH,
MELBOURNE, AND DELHI

Senior Designer	Guy Harvey
Editor	Amy Junor
Publishing Manager	Simon Beecroft
Brand Manager	Robert Perry
Category Publisher	Alex Allan
DTP Designer	Hanna Ländin
Production	Vivianne Cracknell

First American Edition, 2006
Published in the United States by
DK Publishing
375 Hudson Street, New York, New York 10014

06 07 08 09 10 10 9 8 7 6 5 4 3 2 1

ISBN-13: 978-0-75662-242-8
ISBN-10: 0-75662-242-5

Color reproduction by Media Development and Printing Ltd., UK
Printed and bound in China by Leo Paper Products.

ACKNOWLEDGMENTS

The Publishers would like to thank Victoria Selover, Lisa St. Amand, Kristin Moffett, Patrick Flaherty, and Elaine Piechowski at Warner Bros., Paul Donaghy for additional artworks, Jo Walton for Picture Research, Jon Hall, Margaret Parrish, Catherine Saunders and Laura Gilbert.

PICTURE CREDITS

The publisher would like to thank the following for their kind permission to reproduce their photographs:
(Key: a-above; b-below; c-center; l-left; r-right; t-top)
Arcticphoto.com: Bryan and Cherry Alexander 13r, 17r, 41r, 45cra, 46tl, 46cla, 46clb, 46bl; David Rootes 45crb; Frank Todd 45tr; Corbis: Tom Brakefield 45br; Getty Images: Kim Westerskov 21r; US Geological Survey: 33t